FII

Field and Fair

PADRAIC O CONAIRE

translated from the Irish
by
Cormac Breathnach

THE MERCIER PRESS
CORK, IRELAND

Mercier Press
www.mercierpress.ie

First published by the Talbot Press in 1929

This selected edition published by Mercier Press in 1966

This edition © Mercier Press 1966

ISBN 978 1 78117 852 2

Transferred to digital print on demand in 2023.

A CIP record for this title is available from the British Librar

Contents

Translator's Note

This translation is an attempt to give readers of English an opportunity of becoming acquainted – not with Padraic O Conaire's art, which is impossible in a translation, but with the things and thoughts that occupied the mind of that rare genius. As the translation, though not strictly literal, is very close to the original, it will be found helpful to students of Padraic's most popular group of stories.

An Appreciation

Wicklow mud still remained wet on the wheels of that grey-green donkey-cart when it jostled one afternoon from Tir-na-nOg, with Padraic O Conaire, into the heart of Dublin. It was an autumn afternoon more than twelve years ago. And in Grafton Street his black little donkey took its stand where shining limousines had emptied out their ladies for the evening's delight. Rain threatened; therefore, pulling that small and stubborn animal by the bit he tethered it to a lamp standard and striking for a near publichouse Padraic and I renewed our old acquaintance on tall stools, making way for new adventures.

It was not the first time that Padraic O Conaire tramped the country. He leathered through the thirty-two counties from the beginning of the European war, making his bed in woods, in lowly homes and even in jails, where the English lodged him in days of suspicion, after many a one-sided controversy in Gaelic with the old police. And maybe it was from the roads that Padraic O Conaire got his long and heavy stride. It was surely for the roads that he carried his heavy boots and heavy stick – that short, hardy man well made for travel, with a good grip of the ground and a body tough with Connemara bone. He was proud of his physical strength; and why not? I have even seen him, good-humouredly, try his wrestling agilities on a professional boxer; and by a sudden wrench of the ribs from Padraic's embrace, that crafty fighter was floored in a twinkle.

Indeed, that virile and granite land by the Connemara sea was bred into his being. His father came from Garaffin, Rosmuck, and married a woman of the Galway MacDonaghs. Padraic O Conaire was born in March 1881, at 5, High Street Galway; and his first schooling took place at the Presentation Convent in that city. His people, of course, were Gaelic speakers but Padraic, when eleven years of age, went to Garaffin, Rosmuc, where he attended Turlough Beg national school; and there his simple Irish greatly matured. After a sojourn of four years in Garaffin, young O Conaire left Rosmuc. In the meanwhile his education continued at Rockwell and Blackrock Colleges; until in 1899 he left Ireland to take up a minor position in the London Civil Service. And it was in London that the seed of Padraic O Conaire's mind came to flower and to early fruit. There his friendships were with noble fellows, with rough men and with vagabond poets, who lived their poetry and rarely wrote it. Indeed, it was an occasion of necessity that first compelled Padraic to put his pen to literary use; and then, as he often told me, it was to write a story of thrills in English – on the suggestion of his strange friend Thomas Boyd, that vigorous Irish poet who came into O Conaire's life as mysteriously as he left it, and was never heard of again. In London, as in Dublin, Padraic O Conaire had no sympathies with those who were suckling at literary pretence; but his vigorous mind, his humour and his realism did much to wean many from such skim milk. And, as a matter of fact, the buoyancy in his own career of tragedy was that terrible passion for Gaelic life and speech that made him one of the greatest writers creating solely in Gaelic – poorly paid Gaelic; that turned him into a most effective teacher in the London Gaelic League; and that saved him, incidentally, from the possibilities of financial success in English letters. But the burst of war created a new London for Padraic O Conaire; values changed; racial stocktaking was necessary, and in the process Padraic resigned in 1914 from the thinning Civil Service – an event wildly celebrated with his fellow yellow bitterns! He returned to Ireland, to a new Ireland and to one after his own heart. After his return every place west of Dublin and east of Galway became his abode.

Outside the lure of friendships in Dublin, Connemara and its people held his strongest ties. A Connemara-man readily understands such ties and particularly an O Conaire. Padraic was part of that country – with his soft voice, his cold grey eyes well set apart in a broad, tawny face that was clean carved and lean from the slim nose to the strong chin. Even his illuminating talk had got the West in it – every phrase delightfully tanged. It was kindly, exuberant, full of charm, moving through stories of his many experiences – reminiscences partly of fact and partly of imagination – all revealing a queer interest in incidents of strange human traits and the zeal of living. Reminiscences, surely, frequently related to his friends and mostly recorded in his stories. These may be found in Nora Mharcus Bhig, in Deoraidheacht, in An Chead Chloch, in An Crann Geugach, and in Seacht mBuadh an Eirighe Amach – indeed in any of his seven volumes of short stories, his two novels, and his play, Bairbre Rua.

Although he made no poetry in song, one thinks of our old poets and their lives when thinking of Padraic O Conaire; not so much of Raftery, one links him rather with Cathal Buidhe, with the 'Mangaire Sugach', or with Flaithri O Maoilconaire, that noted member of the western bardic family from whose seed Padraic traced his decent. O Conaire was one in whom the proud art of the genealogist was a living faculty. One found in him a survival of the Gaelic attitude towards life: rather fatalistic, dramatic, most realistic, with its keen sense for beauty in beast and being – its wild delicacy, fugitive from some other world, a world mentioned just under the breath. One watched in him in company arguing with a friendly stranger, while behind the screw of an eye he sized up his man with all the shrewdness of a Connemara mind. That shrewdness was inbred in Padraic O Conaire: were not many of his forefathers in the old days traders by sea and land, ropemakers and boat builders in Galway – seafarers bearing hides, timber and wool into the southern ports of Europe and bringing back wine and Spanish merchandise for use among the Connachtmen.

Within his last few years O Conaire moved, even more closely, with his many Connemara friends – wise old women and men, cronies of his, and young people – while teaching Irish in Galway. His ways became legend in that lonely world along the western sea-board. Indeed, he was usually found in strange places, under queer circumstances, and often with surprising companions. One of my last sights of him was caught from the corner of a window in some Galway square as he passed outside and he leading a crowd of neighbouring children; when I left my glass and rushed out to overtake them, he and the children had disappeared. He died in a Dublin hospital on 6th. October 1928; and his possessions were found – just an ounce or two of tobacco, his pipe and an apple. The body of Padraic O Conaire lies in Galway earth; but the hardy flower of Padraic O Conaire's mind is shining for the lowly, the passionate and the knowledgeable stock of the Gael; and with it, his personality is artistically alive – a delight to all lovers of life and of literature.

F.R. HIGGINS.

An Invitation

Come with me, o friend of my heart, and let us enjoy the sight of majestic mountain peaks and dark pine forests; let us stroll by musical streams, past cool brooks where dwell thousands of birds; come along for Spring is at hand, and fresh blood is flowing through your veins and mine. The lambs are bleating and frisking in the fields, the sap is circulating through all living plants, mildness and softness are in every breeze that blows, there is a tender glow from the sun, the skies are clement and the surly winter days with their biting winds are gone.

Get ready, friend of my heart, and come along with me. Leave the city and the city ways; cast away gloom and anxiety and heartache; cast away the sorry rags of life and of long woeful winter. Come along with me and watch the coming of Spring with all its delights and glory. Learn of the birds of the wood, the little animals of the gardens, the insects of the bushes, the trout in his pool, the little timid rabbit, the fleet-footed hare, the hard-fighting badger, the fox, the thorny hedgehog, the brown squirrel on the tree, the otter in the river foam. Come along with me that your sad heart may rejoice, that your spirit may be stirred, that your sadness may be solaced, that we both may welcome Spring and the re-birth of the world. We shall do our exploring chiefly on foot, but we shall also have the little black ass, and all our luggage in the little grey-green car I bought for him, so that if you but cast away all worldly cares and melancholy we shall be going light on our way. The poor ass will not feel his burden. He will have to carry only the things we shall need for our journey – a tent I made myself from the old sail of a boat to keep the dew and damp of the night from us; a box containing food and the means to prepare it; two pieces of the old sail from which I made my tent in order that we may have dry beds for the night. Yes, that is all we shall have with us on the car, except the few little comforts you may happen to bring with you for your own use.

What a time we shall have! The long white road stretched out before us, enticing us and urging us on-ward, the fragrance of Spring arising from the tillage, a soft glow from the sun, a gentle zephyr from the south, laden with the delightful scents of the clay and of sprouting plants, and you and I going along at our ease and at our own good pleasure.

Blossoms of every species will come forth vying with each other in beauty; you will climb craggy cliffs seek-ing the rare kinds you so love; but as for me I shall lie on the grass on the flat of my back by the road-side gazing up at the big amber clouds as the breeze wafts them across the heavens; and I shall study anew and more closely than ever before the ways of the ants and wonder at the strange life the frogs lead in the pool beside me. Have no doubt about it: I shall not be lonely in your absence; but when you return you'll be welcome, and, of course, you'll teach me the name and nature of every little plant you have collected in your explorations.

Then we shall jog along together until noon when I shall select a suitable spot facing the sun, but with the trees shading us overhead; and there we shall spend an hour or two at our ease.

I shall unharness the ass and give him the oat-bag to feed from. I shall turn out my little store for our own meal – bread and butter, cheese and hard-boiled eggs will be our mid-day fare. Come along with me, my friend, and we shall travel until night overtakes us. We shall pass thro' snug little villages with a light in every house, and a merry fire to be seen thro' the open door, and the bean-a-tighe busy preparing the meal, or minding her baby, or having a chat with her neighbour; or should you happen to look into one of the houses as you pass by, perhaps what you see inside will make you lonely, and I may feel lonely too. But the loneliness will not last long – it will vanish like a flash.

And we shall stray onward at our leisure until we reach a certain little pine wood that I know. There we shall spend our first night.

I shall erect the tent on its poles. We shall both gather faggots. I shall kindle a fire at the mouth of the tent, because I know how; but you too may learn that trade as well as everything else pertaining to an open-air life – and remember I shall be very cross with you unless you learn how to kindle a fire with green wood in a damp hollow on a wet day, to make an appetising meal from old bones and a few small potatoes, to pitch the tent, to catch the little black ass in the mornings, to spancel him for the night, to dress the beds, to distinguish good water from bad, and to chant me a lullaby at night whenever I may ask that favour.

I shall teach you all these branches of the wanderer's science. But at first, at all events, I shall kindle the fire myself, fetch in the spring water, cook the food, and dress the beds – wait until you see the two lovely springy beds I shall make from the old sail! You will never wish to lay your limbs on any other.

But I fear you may feel afraid the first night you spend with me in the wood. You'll hear sounds you never heard before. These sounds will come from the wood. There is music in the pine that is in no other tree, faint and melancholy music that the tree gives forth as if it were ever lamenting the dead. Should there be a strong wind you will hear a wonderful noise on the tops of the bare branches – the ghosts and evil spirits of the woods fighting out their battles in the darkness of the night. But if the night be calm you will hear other music overhead, a soft lullaby that would put even a murderer to sleep...

You'll hear the short angry bark of the fox pursuing his prey in the midnight hours, the timid squeak of the rabbit, the scream of the hare, the pitiful wail of some unlucky wood rat caught in a trap and struggling in vain to get free. But it is the birds of the wood that will startle you most – especially when the dawn is near. A little bird – its name I do not know, but its song resembles that of the robin – starts the chorus. But remember this, if you happen to be awake listening to any of the night sounds of the wood, no matter what joy or sorrow you may feel, don't wake me; if you do, believe me you'll hear a sound that is but seldom heard in this or any other wood.

The first ray of light will appear. By degrees the song of the birds will grow louder and more cheerful. We shall arise with music in our ears and even on our tongues. We shall strike into the wood, and if we be in luck we shall return with a fine rabbit for breakfast.

The sun will be high above the horizon before we are on our way again, jogging along without trouble or trial, you and I. And when the heat of the mid-day sun is at its strongest we shall pick out the most suitable spot on which to rest ourselves and eat our midday meal. Thus shall we spend the fine sunny days of Spring.

Up, friend of my heart! Turn your back on the city, forget your troubles and come along with me into the wilderness. I have much to offer you: ease and peace, happiness and pleasure; knowledge of and acquaintance with God's creatures big and little; hospitality and delight – and the south wind that will gladden your heart, however sad you may feel tonight.

Should rain or bad weather or unseasonable frost and snow overtake us, I shall find for you such shelter and cover that you will not know whether the day is wet or dry, whether the night is cold or sultry. There you will shake off the worry and the sorrow of heart that now oppress you.

If at any time you feel very weary or much depressed by the loneliness of the night, we can then, of course, make for some village near by, take our seats beside the fire in one of the inns, drink good Spanish wine, chat with the landlord or some of his customers, and spend the night there if we choose, or resume our journey when we feel ourselves refreshed for another bout of travelling.

Up, friend of my heart, and come along with me until I have cured that dark disease that afflicts your mind. Arise and fare forth by my side, by high majestic mountain peaks, by dark pine forests, by streams that make music all day long, by the banks of cool brooks innumerable where the birds in their thousands dwell and make merry. Delay not, but come along.

My Little Black Ass

It was in Kinvara that I first made acquaintance with my little black ass. It was a fair day and he was standing beside a fence with his back to the weather – heedless of the world, and the world heedless of him. From the first moment that I laid my eye on him I admired him. I wanted an ass, for I was weary of tramping, and wouldn't this little fellow carry myself, my bag, my great coat, and my other knick-knacks? And thought I, I may get him cheap.

I inquired for his owner, but I searched the town before I found him, in front of a publichouse, singing ballads for pennies. What! Sell the ass? Why shouldn't he sell him if he got his value? Yes, his value, and not a penny piece more than his value did he want; and only that the times were so bad he would never part with him – no fear! A fine young ass that could easily cover twenty miles a day. If he got a handful of oats once a month there wouldn't be a racehorse in the land that would hold a candle to him – not a horse!

Together we examined the 'points' of the animal. What praise the owner gave him! There was never another ass, since the first ass came to Ireland, he assured me, so hearty, so sensible, and so far-seeing as he.

'Do you know a habit he has?' said this master of the arts of praise; 'if you gave him a little grain of oats in the morning, he would put some of it to keep, fearing a scarcity next day – by all the holy books in Rome, he would.'

Somebody laughed. The tramp faced him. 'What are you laughing at, you simpleton?' said the tinker. 'He is so wise that he stores away a part of his food; isn't it often I was in such straits myself, that I had to steal from him. Only for that ass it is often my twelve children and myself would be hungry!'

I inquired casually if this wise ass of his could distinguish between his master's and his neighbour's oats.

'He's as honest as the priest,' said the man, 'if all animals were like him, there would be no need for fence or trench, hedge or moat – not the smallest need.'

A huge crowd had gathered round us by this time. The tinker's own children were there – I am not sure if the dozen were present, but the kind of youngsters that were there, you wouldn't meet anywhere else in Ireland. A ragged, dirty, greasy set of children; and each surpassing the others in ill-manners. His wife was there, barefooted, hatless, wild.

'Peter,' she said, 'do you remember the day he swam into the river and rescued little Mickileen, when the stream was sweeping him away?'

'Why shouldn't I remember it?' answered he. 'Yes

Sabby, and you remember the day I was offered five pounds for him.'

'Five pounds,' she said, turning to me. 'Yes, he got five gold sovereigns into the palm of his hand.' 'My soul! I did,' said he, interrupting her, 'the bargain was closed, and the money in my hand –'

'But,' she broke in, 'when he saw the poor ass shedding tears because we were parting with him, he couldn't find it in his heart to let him go.' 'Whist!' said her spouse, 'speak gently, I tell you! There isn't a word we're saying that he doesn't understand. See his ear cocked?'

I bid a pound for this marvellous beast.

'A pound,' yelled the tramp. 'A pound,' screamed his wife. 'A pound!' roared the twelve children all together.

How astonished they became! They gathered round me to see what I looked like. One urchin took hold of my coat; another of my pants. The youngest of them gripped me round the knee. Another hopeful put her hand into the pocket of my trousers; of course the creature was only trying to find out if I had even the pound – but instead of a pound she got a slap under the ear; and it was not from the tinsman she got it.

I liked the little black ass very well. He would suit my purpose. He would carry me part of my road, and I could sell him any time I felt tired of him.

'A pound!' said I again.

'Two pounds,' said the tramp.

'O! O!' wailed the woman, 'my fine ass going for two pounds,' and she broke into sobs and tears.

'For a pound,' I insisted.

'For a pound then – and sixpence to each of the children.'

The bargain was closed at that. I gave him the pound. I also gave sixpence to each of his children who ranged around me. The woman had called them up – Seaneen and Nedeen, and Taimeen, and I don't know how many others. There wasn't a beggarman at the fair who didn't bring his offspring about me, all threatening and screaming. What a din they made! What quarrelling and confusion was on every side of me! One complained that he received no sixpence – though the coin was under his tongue at that moment! Another said – but nobody could know what anybody was saying, or trying to say, there was such a hullabaloo.

Pity it was I didn't give him the two pounds at first, and have nothing to do with those presents to his endless family.

I left the village 'in state.' I was mounted on the ass, the tramp on my right holding the headstall, his wife similarly engaged on my left, the children howling around us.

Some of the village lads followed us, each of them giving me his own bit of advice. The ass was compared to the most famous racehorses of the day. I was cautioned to be on my guard, lest he might take head and disappear for ever. I was advised to give him such and such a kind of food. One would imagine the crowd had never before seen any object to laugh at, until they beheld me mounted on my little black ass, and escorted along by a band of tramps.

But what cared I? Had I not the ass – just the animal I had been wishing to have for many a day! Can I describe how myself and my ass parted company with this roving escort? Each one of them in succession wrung my hand nine times, and each of them spoke caressingly and coaxingly to the ass... His virtues were rehearsed to me, seven times over. A promise was extracted from me that I would be nice and gentle to him, give him a handful of corn whenever I could afford it, give him a wisp of hay at night, and, for the life of me, never, never use the stick on him. Then, as we were parting, a wail of woe was raised. The father began it. The mother helped him, the children followed suit, until soon the woods around me were filled with their heart-rending lamentations...

I was alone at last – alone with my little black ass.

Off he went at a gallop, until we left the wood behind us. I felt I had made an excellent bargain. Where could anybody find an ass so lively, so spirited, as my little black ass?

But when we had got clear of the wood there was a different story to tell. A foot he wouldn't stir, this incomparable ass of mine. I thought to coax him along by flattering words. He didn't heed me. I thought to move him with the stick. Stir he would not; but stood fast there in the middle of the road.

People passed by; they had been at the fair, and were in merry mood. I was advised to do this, and do that; but when one joker advised me to give the ass a lift on my back, my patience gave out, and I threw stones at the ill-natured jester.

At last I had to dismount and drag the ass along against his will. What prayers did I not offer up for the roving rake who had sold me this precious beast!

But soon I observed a peculiar fact. The ass, I could see, was nervous, and the wind playing through the branches of the trees seemed to startle him. As he passed under the arms of the trees that grew by the roadside his laziness at once vanished, and it became almost impossible to hold him in. He would first cock an ear; then he would shake himself as a dog does on leaving the water, and, quick as thought, he would fly ahead like a whirlwind.

I was in luck. I had found out his secret.

I tied him to a gate, went into the wood and plucked an armful of fresh grass and leaves. These I wove into a garland which, as we were leaving the wood, I placed about his neck and over his two ears.

The poor beast! You never saw such speed as he made. He thought because of the music in his ears that he was all the time in the wood. When we arrived in Ballyfeehan all the village turned out to behold the wonder – myself, and that little black ass of mine wearing his leafy crown.

I have the little black ass still, and I shall have him until he dies. Many a long mile we have travelled lonely roads in all kinds of weather. He has mended his ways in some respects. His master, alas, has not; and I believe the little black rogue knows as well as anybody in the world that he has not.

But you have never seen anything so proud as he has become of late, since I bought a pretty grey-green car for him. Growing younger the poor creature is ever since I first tackled him to the car.

The World's Daily Oblation

Was it day? On opening my eyes I saw a large bright star in the heavens over me, a beautiful torch shining down open me between the bare arms of the ash tree which grew beside me. The Milky Way formed a silver road across the sky. A vivid imagination could easily picture hosts of angels travelling along that road. Another star which I did not recognise stood sparkling above the eastern horizon. Something made one feel that it was playing the music of the heavens to which man is deaf because of some defect in ear – or heart.

The bare arms of the ash tree above were stirred; so was every plant and herb about me. You will say it was the wind blowing through the branches that caused the stir; but I have a different idea as to its cause; and have I not as much right to say that it was not a material power – that it was not the wind that caused this movement, as you have to say that it was?

It was as calm a night as you ever saw, without a move in the air, without the slightest sound of faintest noise to be heard until this music began in the branches. If you imagine it was the wind that made the music, would you please tell me why I heard a sound as if thousands of wee men were drawing tresses of finest silk along the grassy surface beneath me? The wind through the trees indeed! you worldly fool!... Another sound!... There was a tall horse chestnut tree on my right, and noises began to come from its uppermost branches.

Something large and heavy was falling and striking against the arms and leaves in its descent. What was it? The music which began in the branches a moment ago had now ceased, and the night was calm, without a sound to be heard, but this noise in the upper arms of the horse chestnut tree – some big, heavy thing falling down from branch to branch slowly and awfully in the stillness of the night... Fear seized me as I lay there in the night under the tree; but it was no earthly fear – no, but terror of some mysterious power which I could not comprehend.

It was falling, ever falling, and the noise gaining strength until I imagined that some angry angel was hurling a star at me because I had not been just to my own soul.

At last the thing fell beside me – fell on a stone. Such a noise as it made in the stillness of the night! And yet what was it? A horse chestnut – the last one on the tree.

A little bird was awakened in a bush near by. The poor creature shook itself; gave a jump from its branch to another branch where it found a place for rest and sleep. I did not see it, but I know I am telling truthfully what happened because it uttered two little squeaks, one on each branch, before it went to sleep again. Another bird, one of the owl tribe that is rarely seen or heard, uttered a barbarous note. He spoke sleepily and wearily in his own dialect just as if he were trying to convey to the beasts and birds of the night his affliction of heart at the fact that his race was now but seldom heard in the land of Ireland. But no heed was paid to his groan nor his woe – no more than was paid to a blackbird in the wood that had just uttered its first note of joy.

And there were many more of the bird tribe that awoke and stirred and made music, each after its kind; but I had no accurate knowledge as to which of the seven score tribes they belonged. I knew only that each one awoke, stirred and spoke after its own fashion; why did they stir, and why did they speak though it was not yet day?

An ass was tied beside me – my own little black ass. He was lying still on the ground. He, too, raised his head and spoke out vigorously. A cow near by bellowed. A foal whinnied. A sheep bleated. I myself felt a sadness over me as of some impending affliction.

And if I had but understood it aright this big strange world was expressing grief. The star above the eastern horizon, the tree that had shed its last nut, the bird that awoke and warbled, the animal that cried weirdly in the night – one and all they were sighing and sorrowing. And the great mighty world –

it too heaved a sigh.

As to myself, I stirred, sighed, and spoke, 'O Great God of Glory!' I ejaculated; and that was all.

Then I realised that I was in the presence of one of the deepest of mysteries, that I was looking at and listening to the world awakening; and it was not the awakening of morning, but the awakening that occurs each night of the year when everything alive on the face of the earth stirs and sighs. At the same hour every night, every herb and bird and beast and human being makes its sign of sorrow – it is the hour at which Lucifer raised his standard in rebellion against God his Creator...

I looked at the star above the eastern horizon; I looked at the tree which had dropped its last nut; I looked where the bird had spoken mournfully on the branch.

'O Great God of Glory!' said the star.

'O Great God of Glory!' said the bird.

And then my heart and soul were stirred to the depths, and with fervour I exclaimed:

'O Great God of Glory!'

And then I fell asleep.

In the Wood

The sun was setting as I reached the wood in my little ass-car, and it did not take me long to select a place to spend the night. It would be hard to find a more suitable spot. There was a murmuring rivulet in which to bathe my feet, and a spring well near by from which to get water for tea; and there was, moreover, the glory of the forest with its great old beech trees re-adorning themselves to greet a new summer, with its dark ash-buds, and its patches of amber light coming and going between the arms of the old trees.

I was very weary. I unyoked the little ass. To prevent his wandering away through the wood in the course of the night, I tied one end of the reins to his right foreleg and the other to the car. Then I made myself a comfortable rocking bed by hanging a piece of old sail-cloth under the car; and to ensure that there would be no 'drop-down' on me, I raised the rest of the sail on poles over the car. No man of the road ever had a bed to surpass mine for dryness and comfort.

I set off and gathered faggots and brushwood, filled my tin-can with spring water, lit my fire at the mouth of my tent and hung the kettle over it. Here I sat on my haunches watching and tending the fire...

There is a special art in kindling a fire in the open air. You must select the small faggots very carefully, and avoid putting any of the soft green wood on until the fire is well, kindled. Otherwise you'll be very soon without a fire. I was fairly expert at this kind of work, and at the end of half an hour I had a fire that would roast an ox.

Whenever I put on a fresh piece of wood I used to close my eyes in order to find out if I could distinguish the various kinds of timber by their smell peculiar to itself; and one skilled in such matters could tell which kind of wood would be burning. But I had not yet advanced to that degree of knowledge – I was but learning.

A better cup of tea than the one I made in the wood that night I had never drunk before. I advise you – most strongly advise you – O reader, to wet your tea in the same manner as I did. Yes, and to drink it in a grove at nightfall.

Boil the water to begin with; then put your tea in a little linen bag, and immerse this bag in the water-can. Don't leave it there too long – two minutes will be sufficient if the water be boiling properly. Take the linen bag out of the vessel, put in your milk or cream and that drink will satisfy you, unless you are one of those people whom nothing can satisfy.

It satisfied me at all events; it would be strange if good tea, bread, fresh butter, and newly laid eggs wouldn't satisfy a roadster like me. Yes, that is a meal good enough for king or heir-apparent, only let him prepare it for himself at nightfall in the middle of a luxuriant wood, with the freshness and the wonder of Spring to gladden his heart.

However it might be with others, I found the taste of honey on every morsel of the food – there was never before such tea drawn, or such bread kneaded, and as for the butter – the taste, colour and smell of it surpassed anything ever produced from cream. Time passed so pleasantly during this royal repast that darkness stole upon me unawares, and when I had finished there were the flames of my fire of wood colouring everything all round me.

To give full vent to my delight I burst into song...

Soon I saw and felt some wonderful things. The fire grew bigger. Long slender tongues of flame shot up, seeking, as it were, to kiss the lower arms of the tree, and no two of these tongues were of the same shape or colour. These flames had colours that were never seen on any rainbow, and an expert, I think, could have told from what species of wood each flame proceeded.

The fierce crackling of the flames would put terror in your heart. If each flame had a particular colour according to its origin, so had it also its own peculiar kind of music, and that music, wild and angry, could be surpassed only by the tongue of a scolding woman...

The music of the various kinds of wood and my

own music and the manner in which the fire threw light all round were no doubt the attraction for the flock of birds that assembled there. I don't think I exaggerate when I say that at least twenty species of them were to be seen there. They sat on the branches of the trees all around, quietly, listlessly. You would have but to rise and stretch out your hand to catch a dozen of them.

But, as for my little black ass – I don't know whether it was sleepy or tired or weak he was; he didn't give the slightest heed to anything about him, but stood there as solemn and as silent as a head-constable in charge of a political prisoner.

I had no desire to sleep, and I remained at the fire until near day-break collecting faggots and pieces of wood, and burning them.

Just at dawn I saw a queer frightened-looking dwarf approach me. I imagined at first it was the demon or evil spirit of the forest coming with a challenge; seldom have I seen a more miserable mis-shapen creature. He was no more than four feet in height, and one would think that if a good blast of wind overtook him it would blow him off the face of the earth. There was terror in his eyes.

'What ails you, man,' said I. 'Have you seen some ghost or apparition that you look so frightened?'

He made no reply. He did nothing but peep cautiously around him; he evidently had no fear of me, for before I had time to put a second question he darted under the little car and hid himself there.

I did not interfere with him. At the end of half an hour or so, I heard a queer little sound.

'For God's sake,' said the dwarf, tremblingly, 'if she comes this way don't tell her where I am.'

I did not know who his pursuer was, but I gave the promise as requested. It was clear day when the pursuer arrived – a terrible woman full of anger... but that is another story, and I shall keep it for another time.

The Awakening

I was so road-weary that I decided to sleep until mid-day, in order to refresh myself. I had not lain on a bed for a month previously, and I was at first rather loth to lie between the cold white sheets. It was the kind of feeling one has before taking the first plunge into the sea on the coming of summer. Going to bed was such a novel sensation that I almost made up my mind not to undress! What a cold, forbidding appearance these white sheets presented! I began to shiver before I jumped in.

But once in, I was at ease. I stretched and again drew in my limbs. I looped myself like an eel. I turned on my right side; then on my left; and then, as if wishing not to lose any of the comfort of the bed, I lay on my back. I drew a long, easy breath – like one who had feasted with royalty. Then I gazed upwards at the ceiling, round at the white walls and across at the two tightly closed windows. I thought I had never slept in a more pleasant place.

Who would sleep in a forest glade or on a lake shore or beside a murmuring brook, however sheltered the places might be, while such shelter as I now enjoyed was to be found nearby in a mountain hut! It is all very well for the poets to sing of dark gloomy forests, of foggy glens, of bright rivers, of starry dark-blue skies, of the golden sunset, of the blackbird warbling in the early morning; but as for me I vowed I would forsake them all henceforth, and would sleep only between white sheets in a small airtight room, having a white ceiling over me, and white walls around me.

How delightful it was to have an opportunity of shaking off my wariness in such surroundings'. Is there any other comfort comparable with it? Do not mention to me the joys of heaven! everybody has his heaven in his own heart; and the heaven of one may not be the heaven of another. But he who cannot enjoy a fine feather bed with white sheets and pillow and bolster must be a bad cantankerous fellow. Place no confidence in him; don't cultivate his friendship or his society. He is not a man of his word...

Beware of the man who prefers starry dark-blue heavens to a pretty ceiling over him, who prefers to lie on the ground underneath a fragrant flowery briar than between two sheets – beware of him. He may be a poet, but nevertheless be on your guard; he will abandon you in your hour of need. That, at all events, was my thought as I lay for the first time in a month between the sheets in my little white room.

I lit my pipe and sent upwards a cloud of beautiful blue smoke, and that smoke assumed more pleasing shapes than ever I beheld on heavenly clouds at the hour of sunrise. I spent a considerable time watching these smoke clouds that wafted so airily above me.

How pleasantly heated my limbs became! Henceforth let no one dilate to me on the heat that comes from the sun as one reclines on a mossy bank in the forenoon, nor on the heat given out by a good fire on a cold night when the earth is frost-bound; mention them not because they are not worth mentioning when compared with the sensation of heat one who has slept for a long time under the canopy of heaven feels in his bones and limbs when lying between two sheets. There is no heat, no pleasure, no bodily comfort to equal that...

Did you ever notice an infant three months old lying nude before a fire! Did you observe how quiet, how satisfied it looks? It stretches its little soft limbs, draws them up, while all the time its half-shut eyes are glistening with joy.

It gives expression to its delight by ejaculating gloo-oo-oo, and by twisting and turning its little body. I felt the joy of that babe as I was shaking off my woe and weariness between the clean white sheets.

And if I didn't make a ball of myself as the naked baby does before the fire, the flesh, not the spirit was at fault.

I became absorbed in thought. Strange fleeting fancies came into my mind; and no sooner would one take possession than it would be ousted by another. They came separately and in groups – stray thoughts that have been since the beginning of time wandering round the world seeking in vain a place in which to take root and grow and increase until they lit on this miserable person lying between unaccustomed sheets.

I struggled valiantly against them. I endeavoured to catch one of them and squeeze the blood and marrow out of it, but it eluded me. I had as little chance of catching a sunbeam.

But no sooner would one be gone than a worse would take its place. I resolved to pay no heed to them, good, bad or indifferent; then they became ever so much bolder and more daring. They were like a host of mocking devils teasing and tormenting me. The day was breaking. Sleep seemed to have deserted me. I almost resolved to forsake forever fine sheets, white walls, snug houses, comfortable feather beds and once again take to the open air – but a wink of sleep came upon me – just one little wink.

I was awakened suddenly.

I turned on my side and listened. It was evident something had struck the window.

'Heavy rain,' I said to myself, 'but let the brown rain pour down in torrents, for I'll not get out of bed to-day,' and I pulled the bed-clothes more tightly about me.

I started to count lest sleeplessness should again assail me. It did not, I fell asleep. Again the noise at the window! What was it? I was too lazy to rise, almost too lazy to open my eyes; but I could not help listening.

One cannot estimate time in one's sleep; I do not know what time had elapsed when the noise came again. But it came. I watched...

Somebody was throwing sand at the window in order to awaken me. I can assure you I did not give that person my blessing

I heard a woman's voice outside. I recognised the voice, and as soon as I did I jumped out of bed; but I vow to you that no other earthly sound could entice me from my fine bed at that early hour.

But that woman! Who would fail her?

Fifty Years a Widow

Who should come in but the widow! She looked younger than I had seen her look for many a day; nobody would imagine that she was over seventy-five years of age and eligible for the old-age pension, or that her daughter and grand-daughter, who lived with her, were also widows.

'Yoke the ass,' she said.

I obeyed without question. One could easily see that she was bent on some strange adventure. There was a slight glow on her old wrinkled cheeks, and a peculiar light in her eyes. I have seen the same kind of light in the eyes of a schoolgirl bent on mischief. I did not question the old lady concerning the cause of her mirth. I knew her better than that, and was well aware of the difficulty of getting her secret – but Time would tell me all.

We both set out in the ass-car, she with her heart full of some secret pleasure. The country around was rejoicing with us. The yellow autumn sun was rising, causing glen and plain to resemble a golden lake, and the roadside tree a golden image, casting beams of golden light on branch and bough and leaf in such a manner that one would imagine the gold age had come.

The ass was in a trot. That wonderful autumn

morning scene delighted me; the old woman was delighted too – but why was she so? considering the life of worry she had led – and was leading.

And certain it is that if she were not so lighthearted her life would be a life of woe. Her husband had died before reaching his thirtieth year; her sons had wandered away she knew not whither; her daughter and grand-daughter were widows – three widows in one house – a house of distrust and dissension.

But that she had plenty worldly means I suppose she would not be even as happy as she was.

I observed her closely as we sat side by side on the ass-cart on that golden autumn day. She was in her Sunday attire, a black silk gown, a black hooded old-fashioned cloak, frilled bonnet, gold rimmed spectacles, but one would scarcely notice these because of her laughing mouth, her cheerful countenance and her excited manner.

We passed her house, and one could easily know by her that she did not wish to be seen in the little ass-car. She had an old umbrella which she opened over her so that she would not be recognised, but the poor woman forgot for the moment that the old umbrella was known to everybody in the parish.

'I believe we weren't seen,' she said, as we were almost past the house.

'Certainly not,' I replied. But I didn't state that I was sure we were seen if anybody happened to be at the window.

At this most inopportune moment it struck the ass that he had trotted far enough for one day. He lowered his head, shook his scraggy little tail, and stood stock still in the middle of the road.

I stood up in the car and vigorously threatened him with my stout blackthorn stick. He merely moved his ears, but declined to move his legs. The old woman stood up and proceeded to urge him with her umbrella. Our united efforts failed; we took counsel.

'We had better walk,' she said.

'Have we a long way to go?' I inquired.

'You'll know that time enough,' she replied; and she pressed her lips closely together lest she might be tempted to divulge her secret.

We were about to dismount when the ass suddenly seemed to change his mind. He shook his head, waved his ears, moved his legs, and went off at a gallop.

Because of the speed of the ass I was unable to attend to the merry old woman beside me, but I knew that her heart was stirred, and that she was enjoying the ride immensely. Her heart was as young on that yellow autumn day as it was any day for fifty years. If you saw us both in the little ass-car, she with her arm round my waist to save herself from falling, her Sunday bonnet sent awry over her left eyebrow by the motion of the car, a smile on her lips, a laugh in her eye, the country around laughing with us – if you saw us you would imagine that I was abducting her!

What fun and sport we had! What cheer and excitement, I and the merry old woman who had been for over fifty years a widow.

She wispered to me. 'I am going to do something this day that I haven't done for fifty years, something I thought I should never do again. I feel hearty and full of courage to-day. A return of my youthfulness...'

We had arrived at the gate of a cornfield. She desired me to pull up the ass. I did. We dismounted.

The corn was in stacks. She asked me to load the car. I proceeded to comply with her request while she, full of excitement, helped me.

I knew that the corn belonged to her daughter, that it was part of the legacy bequeathed to her by her lately deceased husband. But what was the old woman about? Were there not plenty of workmen in the homestead to fetch a load of corn if it were needed? And what did she mean by saying she was going to do 'something she hadn't done for fifty years?'

The car was loaded. We made for the gate. The ass wished to turn home, but she prevented him.

'Whither bound?' I inquired.

'To the market,' she said, 'to Killowen to sell this corn.'

I was astonished. She did not need money, and yet here was a woman, rich and proud, going to market to sell a wretched little load of corn. What did she mean at all? Why had she been so excitable all day?

I was in a quandary...

We sold the corn.

She invited me to a hostel. She was known in the place, and we were ushered into a private room. Two glasses were placed before us. She tasted the wine; then became meditative: 'Fifty years – just fifty years to-day! Isn't it a long period!'

She became silent. I did not interrupt.

'I haven't done the like for fifty years,' she said, as if talking to herself, 'and I thought I should never do it again! To steal and sell a load of corn and spend the proceeds in a hostel with a man...'

She looked sharply at me.

'And you have a very strong facial resemblance to him – but he was a handsomer man... my man... fifty years to-day – we weren't married then – we went off to the market with a load of corn. We spent the price of it in this house... I thought I should never do the like again... but this morning when old memories came back to me I became young.'

She took my hand. There was a tear in her old eye.

'For fifty years! God be with the day, and God rest his soul.' 'Amen,' I said.

'You are like him, very like him,' said the old woman in a trembling voice. I did not speak. She squeezed my hand, and looked sorrowfully back over the years...

A Forest Feast

When the old lady left me alone in the wood I began working my very best so that I should have the two trees cut down before her return. Didn't I work! The saw I fetched in the morning was but a poor one; certain it is that if I had known I should have such work to do I would have brought a better tool – but such a cutting contraption as that was! I am unable to reckon the many mighty maledictions I hurled at it ere I was one half hour in the wood. I took off my coat – and my boots, because the place beneath me was a swamp. I tightened my belt, I folded up my shirt sleeves, I bared my breast, I took my stance firmly. I was in a state of perspiration before I had the old saw an inch into the hard timber.

There is little that I wouldn't do to oblige the same old lady. Should she ask me to give battle to the three-headed monster, or to pay a visit to the savage islands in the frozen sea, or perform any other deed of valour and daring it is certain I should undertake it willingly – but to be left alone in the middle of a dense wood oozing perspiration at every pore trying to cut down two stout trees with a worthless saw! And I didn't know under heaven why she asked me to undertake that difficult job; or to what use she would put the wretched trees when I should have them felled.

I am by nature a lazy man. I much prefer to sit on the fence watching the hurlers rather than take part in the game; I feel happier standing in the forge observing the smiths at work than I would were I one of them. I take more delight in lying on my back on a soft mossy patch on a sultry summer day having nothing whatever to do but watch the big amber clouds rolling past above me than in any work you could give me. My affection for the noble old lady who set me to fell the trees will be evident when I state that I spent an hour at least without resting, without drawing a calm breath, without bathing a hot swollen hand, but cutting and sawing unceasingly.

Such a heat as I was in! I never before perspired so freely, and I never will again, no matter what any woman may ask me; but the modest, majestic old lady of whom I was so fond I never failed her, and I never will as long as God spares me my health.

But if I only knew why I had been set that task!

I worked for two hours, and with every effort I made with the saw I was growing weaker. I was spent, exhausted. I was scarcely able to stand. I threw away my cutting implement and examined my handiwork. I plucked a trahneen and inserted it in the slit I had made in the trunk. Four inches! – that was the depth of the cut after all my exertions. And there were at least twelve inches more ahead. I lost heart. I wouldn't be able to fell these two trees were I to spend the whole day on them. Yet, I should be for ever disgraced if I were unable to perform this work for the old lady to whom I had given such affection.

I was anxious to resume work and not desist until I had one of the trees felled. If I didn't do that, and I admit I didn't, it was not the spirit but the flesh that was at fault. There was a grassy knoll beside me. I cast away my tools and lay on my back on the knoll to rest myself... It was delightful to be there looking up through the green foliage on the blue sky, and having nothing in the world to do – yes, with nothing in the world to do, because a person cannot rest peacefully unless he can persuade himself that neither he nor anybody else in this world has got a job to do; anxiety is a foe to peace of mind. I routed that enemy as I lay on my back on the grassy knoll. One would not imagine that there was a tree to be cut nor anything else to be done on that fine sultry day.

I wanted an excuse, a good excuse, so that I would not be obliged to lose any more perspiration. Near me was a deep hole with some water at its bottom; if I let the wretched saw slip down into it I would not have to do another stroke of work for the day – but then my dear old dame would be without her trees. I also thought of winding my handkerchief round my hand and pretending I had hurt it – but that trick was as shallow as the first one. My heart sank within me when I pondered on the devilish job I had before me.

There was a cluster of ants busily working beside

me. They were endeavouring to bear off a white withered blade of grass about two and a half inches long. There was a great host of them present, and each was doing its best. What a struggle there was! Didn't they work with a will! I almost gave a shout of congratulations when they succeeded in lifting up the trahneen and carrying it along.

'You ought to be ashamed of yourself,' the reader will say, 'for being so lazy and sluggish.'

I was neither ashamed nor distressed, and I don't see why I should have been. I thought and imagined from the first that the work was a visitation from God, and that it would be a good deed to leave part of it undone; but no sooner had I begun to indulge this reverie than I was suddenly startled.

I heard the voice of the old woman in song coming from the west. I was unable to see her because of the trees, but I jumped up quickly and set to work industriously. One would imagine that, as a sawyer, I was unrivalled.

What power you had over me, O noble lady!

She was beside me before I raised my head.

'And you are working since,' said she.

'At my best,' said I, wiping the perspiration from my brow with the back of my hand.

Then I stared. The old lady was not alone, but was accompanied by a comely young woman whose bright eyes were twinkling with merriment.

I was astonished that I was not introduced to the young lady. The old lady thought, I assumed, we were already acquainted – indeed I knew the young lady by appearance, and was deeply in love with her for two years; but she always avoided me.

'And we brought some food and drink also,' said the old woman, 'and we shall have a feast here in the forest.

There was a large basket on the ground between them, and I was much surprised when it was opened; it contained the maturest drinks and the freshest foods. I should but tantalise you if I were to enumerate the sweets, the rich foods and the strong drinks that were in that basket.

Whilst the young maiden and I were unpacking them the old lady was conversing with herself in an undertone:

'A sunny day, a sultry day like this, the man I afterwards married and myself first came into this wood. And we had a feast together... he and I – but there was an old woman with me – but she was wise, and she left us as soon as the feast was over...' She sighed.

'Fifty years is a long spell,' said she, quietly, 'but I hope I have as much sense to-day as she had that day.'

So she had, because no sooner was the feast over than the old woman slipped away.

The man who would not humour such a shrewd wise old woman could not be called a man at all.

The old Quarry

I recently made my abode in an old quarry on the
bluff of a hill, where there was neither friend nor
fugitive to disturb me. I was not long there till I made
several friends. I became intimate with the denizens of
the quarry, both large and small, with the bold little
robin, with the wee, wee wren, with the yellow-billed
blackbird, with the speckled thrush, with the spright-
ly sparrow; and I used to protect them all from the
voracious hawk when they assembled to pick up the
crumbs of my mid-day meal. An old owl that had the
sense of the seven sages in his head was there, though
he never spoke unless there was great need for his doing so; but no bribe would entice the old philosopher
to leave the hole in the tree where he spent his life.

As to the other birds of the place they were not the
slightest bit afraid of me after I had spent some time
amongst them. Indeed, judging by the manner in
which they used to gather round me, each with its
own song, one would suppose that I, too, was of the
race of beaks and feathers, or, at least, that I was
closely related to that race.

There were four-footed animals also in the quarry,
a squirrel dwelt in the high trees behind the quarry,
a shy stoat with a long, helpless family lived in a heap
of stones; a variety of rat, which frequents only re-

mote places, had a nest in a bush in which he and his spouse were rearing a family of five; and a timid rabbit, with whom the sunlight seemed to agree as little as with the owl, had his abode there.

These four-footed animals caused me most trouble. They were not all disposed to be friendly until I had spent a considerable period in the quarry; but gradually we became neighbourly.

I began with the rabbit – and I must relate exactly how I became intimate with that bashful little fellow, and with the others also; if I do not nobody will understand how it distressed me afterwards to be obliged to make war upon them.

After I had made friends with the feathered clans I set about coaxing the rabbit. I observed that he never left his burrow at night until I had entered my sleeping sack, and if I remained about he would never appear, being too timid – indeed many is the night he went supperless for this reason.

One evening I had lettuce for tea, and I left a few leaves at the mouth of the burrow to wheedle him out.

He came. He first put out his snout as if he were sniffing around. Immediately his well-shaped head and erect ears were protruded; he looked around exactly as if he were asking himself if he had sufficient pluck to venture forth while the sun was yet in the heavens.

He saw the lettuce leaf and began to eat it at his ease, but he had not consumed the entire leaf when he assumed a running attitude. He apprehended the approach of an enemy. But there was no cause for alarm, and he resumed his meal, keeping a good lookout the while. Fresh lettuce leaves! Surely he had not had such a supper since he came to live in the quarry.

I had lettuce on the following night also – and I did not purchase it. I left a few leaves mid-way between the burrow and the sleeping-bag. I was in the grass-coloured bag, but I had a good view of the poor creature as he emerged from his hole, while he was entirely unaware of my presence. He ate the lettuce he found near his burrow. He ate that which was mid-way between the burrow and my bag; then he became daring and started to frolic about the quarry. It was the good rare food that perhaps gave him heart and hope! On another night he came to the mouth of my sack and snatched a leaf of lettuce which was lying on the grass; and every succeeding night he came as fearlessly as if I were merely a tree-trunk.

At first I used to be much surprised on awaking in the morning to find him at the mouth of the bag eating my food. Very soon he was a most perfect pet.

As to the stoat: I was afraid of her at first, because of the stories I had heard about her species in my youth: how she would spit poisonous saliva at a person, how she would grip him by the throat and not let go until she had drawn the last drop of blood;

about the golden purse she keeps in her nest – but everybody has heard these stories. I, however, believed them; yet she is a nice pleasant little animal provided one is properly disposed towards her. She was never as friendly with me as with the rabbit, but she used to come and eat from my hand.

I have mentioned the rat; we were never good friends; on no account would he allow me to lay my hand upon him; but he used to pay me a visit and spend some time sitting on my sleeping sack while I lay inside it.

The squirrel was the most unfriendly of all. Perhaps she considered I was too intimate with her hereditary enemies, the rat and the stoat; anyhow she would not come within yards of me until at last I succeeded by a bribe. I was in the city one day and purchased two pence halfpenny worth of hazel nuts. I broke some of them between my teeth and threw one to the squirrel. She was much astonished, and looked as if she meant to retire to the tops of the high trees never to return – that was her first intention. But that hazel-nut coaxed her; apparently it was very sweet... she commenced to chew it.

It was borne in upon me while cultivating the friendship of the inhabitants of the quarry that each tribe of them is as susceptible to a bribe – provided it be suitably chosen – as a police constable or a county councillor.

It was a droll life we had in that quarry, myself and the animals, once we became closely acquainted.

But alas, it did not last long.

I used to leave my food, bread and meat, tea and sugar, as if I were leaving it in heaven, never suspecting the presence of a thief or vagabond.

One day during an absence of only five minutes half a loaf had disappeared. And the price of bread! That thieving stoat, thought I, I must chastise her. On another occasion I put all the food, except a little cabbage I had procured for my dinner, into the bag: I had no notion, when I set out to get a few pounds of bacon to put in the pot with the cabbage that the latter would have disappeared on my return – but it had.

Shame on you, pilfering rabbit, said I, what a rascally thief you are to deprive me of my food, considering how neighbourly we have been from the first. But wait! You'll get your deserts from me!

I had to go to town one day, but before setting out I carefully stored all the food I had into the bag and hid it under a bush where the keenest human eye that ever was would fail to observe it. I expected, naturally, that it would not be touched, and that I should find everything exactly as I left it, on my return.

Alas! When I got back I found a hole in the bag – my beautiful sleeping-bag, value for twelve shillings, ruined in one day! – the meat it contained was spoiled; there was not left of the bread but the crust;

the thieves had consumed even the sugar.

I poured my maledictions on them all, on the stoat and on the squirrel, on the rat and on the rabbit, and I swore seventeen oaths that I would be revenged on them one and all...

The rabbit was little welcome when he came in the morning, wearing such an air of innocence as if he had never committed a fault. He supposed, I dare say, that I was in a merry mood when I took hold of him – but when I twisted his neck...

Not one of them seemed to realise that I had declared war upon them – but I had!

The Hill of My Heart

With my heart full of joy I struck out through the Vale of Glendalough. It was two or three hours before dawn, but there was plenty of light from the moon and stars, a delightful eerie light that filled the Glen. There lay the two silvery lakes encircled by lofty moonlit mountain peaks; there stood the old churches and the round tower in the distance resembling a vision one might see in a dream...

I made my way past the tower in the old graveyard, and as I heard the wind moaning in the branches above me I pulled my great coat more tightly about me, lengthened my steps somewhat – and, but that I am bound to keep strictly to the truth, I should say that I was seized with terror, and took to my heels.

Such was not the case.

Entranced, I proceeded leisurely between the two lakes, then took the path along the northern shore of the western lake. There was no bird nor beast, nor even insect, but was sleeping silently. I gazed across the lake at the spot where St. Kevin made his bed; he must have been a poet, a great poet, who selected such an abode – and who knows but that Kathleen too had the gift of poetry and selected the same spot ere she became aware of Kevin's presence.

Had I met an old pagan, or abbot, or saint, from the past, I should not have been surprised; were they not all around me, had I but eyes to see them? Was I myself not like one enchanted, who, having thrown off the worries and anxieties of this world, was proceeding through a delightful old world from which had been cast out all evil and malice?

When I reached the head of the glen I looked eastward on the grand panorama beautified by God and man. The wondrous glory of the scene almost frightened me. I said a prayer.

But soon I had to recollect myself. The path that leads westward over the mountain is extremely rugged, and it was with great difficulty that I made my way. Were it not for my previous knowledge of the place I would have been obliged to give up and rest in a cleft of rock until day-break. That would have much distressed me because I had resolved to be on the summit of the highest peak before dawn in order to watch the sun rising from the eastern sea.

I frequently staggered and stumbled but my anxiety to reach the summit in time overcame all obstacles, and I held on my course. Though the night was rather cold I was perspiring freely and as to weariness... my legs were staggering under me most of the time; now and then I used to catch the drowning man's hold of a tuft of coarse grass, or a bunch of heather to help me to climb some crag as steep as a wall. Sometimes I would slip down a few fathoms, and only the fact of my being from youth an expert climber saved me from breaking my bones.

I came upon a bird's nest. Up rose the hen into the dark-blue heavens filling the wilderness as she soared aloft with her mournful complaining notes. By what right did such as I invade her peaceful territory at that hour of night?

There is no knowing what a man might do when he is alone at night on the side of a mountain. I stood on the top of a rock looking after the bird that was passing out of sight and telling her why I had come that way...

My mind suddenly turned to the thin, spare red-haired Sassenach, the witty talkative man whom I had met the previous night in the Glen hotel, and I began to imagine what he would say were he aware that I had left my snug bed in the middle of the night to go to the top of a high hill to see the sunrise.

The moon went down, multitudes of stars were extinguished, it was very cold and calm; I was alone on the summit before the dawn.

I do not know even now the name of the hill, and little it matters; I shall never call it by any name but The Hill of My Heart. There is a cairn on its summit; I added a stone to it, and then I sought shelter where I could rest and take food and observe the daily miracles of nature: the day breaking, light gradually overcoming darkness. I was thankful that I had brought plenty of bread and meat, and very thankful that there was a 'little drop' left in the bottle. I needed it...

God began his daily miracle..

At the eastern horizon a keen eye could discern a little brightening. It was as if little drops of light were being shed from the stars and spread upon the ocean of darkness slowly causing it to whiten. If you closed your eyes for a moment you would on re-opening them observe a new brightness, not alone over the eastern horizon, but all around you. The rock or the bush which a moment previously appeared black and warning was gradually assuming its natural shape and colour.

A mountain bird began to chant; or better, perhaps, say to complain at being aroused so early.

I saw the green sea – I often saw the same colour on the face of a corpse; the amber clouds that overhung the eastern horizon soon began to assume a purple colour; soon, too, the colour of the sea changed to silver.

A golden arrow arose from the silver sea and pierced the clouds. Another and another arrow in quick succession, yet each distinct and separate...

I could clearly see a bird in the clear heavens ready to burst his heart with joy. A golden lake which appeared in the clouds over the sea became bronzed and then reddened before my eyes.

The King of Day himself came swiftly and majestically out of the ocean, the world was filled with his splendid light, my heart was filled with delight and love.

I heard singing beside me – a pleasant human voice in song. I jumped up quickly and looked around to find out who my companion was at sunrise on that mountain summit. There on the top of the cairn stood a thin spare red-haired man singing to his heart's content a noble English song of welcome to the sun.

It was the Sassenach whom I had met in the Glen hotel; he seemed enraptured. When he had concluded his song he addressed me: 'Two poets at sunrise on a mountain top –' and in vain I sought to convince him that I was no poet.

The Gallows Tree

A couple of months ago I was travelling within fifty miles of Dublin. I had no mode of conveyance but my little ass-cart; and my poor ass and myself were in ill-humour because of the oppressive heat of the day. Sometimes he would cover fifty yards of the road like a doe – gadflies and other insects urging him on; at other times he would be loath to put one leg past another, but would keep moving his head up and down, up and down, like a child's doll. No man in Ireland could get him to move when that fit of laziness seized him. I gave him the stick; I addressed him in fair language and foul language; I repeated my seventeen latest oaths in his ear; I sought to coax him with poesy, with whistling, but if I were at him to this day he would not accept advice or urge from me.

I gave him his head and let him proceed in his own strange slow way.

It is rarely my little black ass and myself are of one mind, but when we reached a large tree growing by the roadside we both had but one idea, to seek its shade to rest and recuperate.

We did so. I unyoked the ass. I gathered faggots, kindled a fire and placed on it a can of spring water. I lay on my back at my ease gazing at the thick foliage above me. The tree was an elm, and I never saw one greater in girth and height. Some of its arms were as stout as the trunk of any oak tree I had ever seen in my native place; and the leaves were so thick that the sky was not visible through them. I was in a cool shade, I had the makings of a good meal on the fire, my pipe was full of fragrant tobacco, yet I was not comfortable. I was growing uneasy about something, but I did not know what it was.

I tried to put my grief to flight but failed. It seemed to me there was something eerie in the place; that the tree above me was enchanted, that it was there from the beginning of time, that it would stand there until the end of time, that it had mastery over all that were or would be born.

The tree was my master. Twice I endeavoured to quit the place, but could not. I was held there; the tree had a hold of me while it told me of its great age, its giant trunk, of what friendish deeds it had witnessed.

I did not pay patient attention to the story of the tree.

I would lean on an elbow and gaze into the fire in the hope that the story of the tree would not increase my sorrow and melancholy; but I could not remain long in that position. The tree used to cause me to look at it, to think of it, and to listen to it; its age, its height, its majesty, its comeliness of foliage, its hardness, its excellent shade, the wonderful things with that tree.

A man was passing by – a withered, whiskered and bent old man leaning on two sticks; but that one knows that an old man could not be as ancient as an old tree, one would imagine the man to be as old as the elm.

I bade the old man the time of day. As he answered these, so that I became of one mind and of one soul that happened beside it – the tree informed me of all he opened his dribbling mouth revealing toothless gums:

'That tree,' said he – and one would swear he was the ghost of the tree, 'that tree is older than anything that lives on the land of Ireland to-day. It is called the Gallows Tree.'

'The Gallows Tree?'

'Yes.· Hundreds were hanged on that stout arm above you. In the year '98 my grandmother saw eight men swinging from it one fine summer morning. They presented a dreadful spectacle, each with a rope round his neck. It is often she told me...'

I did not stay to listen to his grandmother's tale. I gathered up all my possessions, yoked my little black ass, and set out on my journey accompanied by the withered, bent and toothless old man.

The Gallows Tree... eight hundred years old.. a tree ere Norman put foot on the soil of Ireland. The oldest live thing we have – is it to be wondered at that you frightened and enchanted me, O tree, while I tried to cook my food and rest myself under your big diabolical arms?

Some time a little later I was in the same district. Sorrow and melancholy had kept me awake for two nights, and since the weather was inviting I went for a stroll about midnight. I traversed bogs and bawns, high roads and mountain paths and I did not rest until I was seated under the tree – under the Gallows Tree.

What power of witch craft have you over me, O Gallows Tree? I praise your stateliness, your great age, your girth and your height; I bow down in reverence to you, O ancient devilish tree, because of the hundreds of men who were hanged from you! I don't praise your produce, O tree; release me and don't inveigle me here again, O steadfast tree...

It was a moonlight night. The withered leaves of the tree were under my feet; the district round glistened like a silver lake under the light of the moon; the air was motionless; the birds on the branches were silent; not a sound was to be heard from any living animal; the whole world was laden with the beauty and enchantment of the night...

I stood up. As I moved the withered leaves and faggots beneath me began to creak in a mournful kind of manner. For a while I paid no heed to this dolorous chant, but kept pacing up and down trying to solve my own difficult problem.

By degrees I began to grasp the meaning of the strange music of the withered leaves under my feet. They appeared to have got the gift of speech, and this was their message:

'We are the produce of the Tree; we are the ghosts of the diabolical Gallows Tree; we are the ghosts of those who were hanged from its arms.'

Terrified I looked around me. The shadows cast by the moon might have been responsible for it, or they might not, but at all events, I imagined I saw a corpse hanging from every stout arm of the Gallows Tree...

I slipped away from the place...

Either on that evening or the following morning I had a conversation with an intelligent man who lived in a village hard by the Gallows Tree 'Those strange sights are frequently seen there,' he stated, 'and it is said that Ireland will never be happy until that same accursed tree is down.'

'Why is it not cut down?' said I.

'That would avail nothing,' he said, 'it must fall of itself.'

The Gallows Tree down! That tree that has weathered the storm of eight hundred years, if story-tellers and botanists – and they are of one word – speak truly; the topmost leaf of that stately tree prostrate on the ground!

The last night on which myself and my little ass-car took that road I failed to reach the village as I had intended.

The first time I went that way the gallows tree hindered me because I had to seek its shade from the heat of the day; on the second occasion it hindered me because it lay across the road.

There was a gang of silent men at work with saws and hatchets and axes on the stout old trunk of that tree – cutting it, splitting it, and trimming it; every man was stripped to his shirt, and was working by torch-light, not a sound was there except that of the large sharp-edged saws lopping off the arms and eating their way into the big trunk.

It was a wonderful sight to watch them working there in the blackness of the night as vigorously as if they were wreaking vengeance on some old enemy.

The queer light used caused all there – man and tree and cutting instruments – to look twice their natural size.

The bearded toothless old man was there – he whom I met on the day the Gallows Tree put me under a spell.

'It wasn't felled, but blown down,' he said. 'And no more was it the hand of man overthrew it – the hand of God did the work. It fell last night: what a terrible storm it must have been to knock down an eight-hundred-year-old-tree?'

I examined the Gallows Tree at the point where

it was divided into two parts; it would be possible to bore a hole thro' it sufficient to accommodate my little ass-car. As to the large arm from which men used to be hanged, it was lying there by the road-side, and school children riding upon it.

The old man with the beard chased them away.

He then addressed me:

'Ireland will be prosperous now,' said he, 'since that old villain is down,' and the old man struck a vicious blow on the ancient tree, as if he were striking a live enemy.

Late that evening I read in the paper that a man had left the shores of Ireland to cross to his own country – a man who deserved neither the thanks nor blessing of our race: the passing of the man and the falling of the tree – who will say that the two events were not connected?

The Blackwater Trout

I would know that trout from any trout that ever looped himself in a river pool. He is older and stouter than most of his relations. And as to his sense! He has tormented the fishermen of the surrounding seven parishes for many a year; every form of bait that ever adorned a hook has been tried on him, but the warrior trout simply sticks out a pointed snout from underneath his rock, mockingly wages his tail and leisurely proceeds on his way.

You can observe him any day in the clear water while he appears utterly indifferent to you or your bait, though excellent it may be. And how tantalising it is to see him rise to seize a live fly of the same colour and appearance as the fly you have on your hook! That clever old trout has elicited many a curse from fishermen in his time! You are a fisherman and would like to try your hand on him? I shall direct you to him: First go to Armagh, and find out any fisherman in that city. Tell him that you heard all about The Trout, and that you are determined not to leave the place until you have him in your bag.

You will be made welcome; you will be told many stories concerning fishermen who came from foreign countries to coax the Blackwater Trout.

You will be introduced to everybody in the town,

young and old, who tried to catch The Trout.

Each of them will show you his own fishing tackle – rod, line and fly. He will tell you of the weight, size and cleverness of The Trout, and will be prepared to lay you a wager that there is not all the fishing stories to be found in books one to surpass that of the Blackwater Trout.

Did not a young man once come from Scotland and swear that he would not leave the brink of the river until he got The Trout! The foolish young man! He was not aware of the wiles of that fish.

He spent the Spring there in a hut of clay and wattles, getting his food sent to him every day from town. Summer arrived. He and The Trout became better acquainted; and as the golden summer advanced they became quite friendly, so that each knew the other's mind.

An old man informed me that it was not fishing but composing poetry the young man spent his days: but who could believe one who never baited a hook?

The place where The Trout dwells is certainly calculated to inspire the gift of poetry; bright running water tumbling over round green stones, a dark, gloomy pool underneath a high mound; that pool delightfully mirroring every cloud and bird that crossed the heavens over it; gently sloping banks covered with variously coloured flowers on both sides of the pool.

And as to the birds that dwell there!

It is said that in no place else in Ireland are swallows so numerous – hundreds and hundreds of them may be seen at eventide skimming merrily over the dark waters.

At the beginning of summer the bushes are filled with the conversation and disputations of each tribe of them. The birds of Ireland hold conference here – a conference as noisy as any other; and I am not sure but that their noise has as much sense; it has, at all events, more melody.

Beside the pool is a grove – a most pleasant place in which to spend a sultry summer day. There you have the buzz of bees, the fragrance of earth and herb and tree, enchantment for him who is capable of being enchanted.

I long for summer – I long deeply for summer and that lonely grove.

I advise the poet to visit that place, to see the dark gloomy pool, the crystal running water, the flower-covered banks with their thousands of birds, the sweet fragrant grove – and The Trout that reigns over this enchanting kingdom.

But I never laid eyes on The Trout, nor on the black pool nor on the crystal water. Yet though I saw them not with my bodily eyes I saw them with that of my mind...

This is how I first came to know of the place and The Trout; as I sat on a little stool in my prison cell dejectedly looking through the window at a patch of azure in the heavens, and observing a swallow that sometimes flew between me and that patch of blue, the door was opened and a keeper entered. It was eventide, and he was at leisure. He opened a pocket-book and produced about twenty fly-hooks.

'You are a trout fisher,' he said. 'I saw in the office some of the flies that were found on you when you were arrested.'

I replied that I took a keen interest in trout fishing. He then asked me to select the best from amongst his own hooks. I did so, and praised some while I dispraised others of his stock. He realised that I had fished and was an expert at the business. The two trout fishers became friends in that prison cell. He lamented my not being able to accompany him that evening in his attack on the Blackwater Trout.

He came to my cell two or three times a week from that time forward. He related to me many stories concerning The Trout and his adventures, with the result that I came to know not only this clever trout, but the dark gloomy pool where he resides, the floral banks, the bright-running water and the enchanting grove.

I could distinguish The Trout from any other that ever swam in a pool; and since Spring is coming with its lengthening days I shall pay a visit to his dwelling-place. I shall make a little hut of clay and wattles on the delightful flower-strewn bank, and shall live alone there like the young Scot; and even if I do not succeed in catching The Trout I may catch some of the poetry of the place.

Farewell, Friends!

Now that genial smiling Summer is gone and Winter cold, wet and dreary is at hand, I must bid farewell to a great many of my old friends, the inhabitants of wood, of wilderness and secluded retreats, and turn my face towards snug abodes until the cold and frost have gone.

And how lonely I am at having to forsake the old quarry for the city! Warm beds, smooth white sheets, the happiness and luxury of the city – how shall I accustom myself to such things after having spent three-quarters of a year under the canopy of heaven. Dear old quarry, I shall never forget you! I shall never forget those ties of friendship forged between myself and my fellow-creatures while I resided in that delightful place. I shall remember to my dying day those starry nights I spent there with nothing between me and heaven but whatever layer or mantle of air envelops this earth of ours. I never thought any of those nights too long, though frequently I had not a wink of sleep from evening twilight till dawn of day; how could I with such companions as I had there? Wasn't it there I became intimately acquainted with the squirrel, the weasel, and with the timid little rabbit?

I made your acquaintance, my dear hairy friends,

while I dwelt alone in the old quarry. I got to know you and your day and night habits, and if estrangement came between us – because of the thieving of the weasel – which of you think I alone was to blame?

And, O feathered tribes, I must bid you farewell and thank you, both songsters and mutes, for your many favours for the past year.

Don't blame me for forsaking you. Alas! that man cannot spend the winter with his summer friends; and though your native haunts are briar and bush and brushwood, the harsh winter goes hard with you, O race of beaks and feathers!

Farewell, friends, until spring comes again, followed by golden summer. And listen, who knows but that I should steal a grain of oats from some farmer and fetch it to you during the winter.

And little black ass: I suppose I must bid you, too, farewell. Here comes cruel winter, and neither of us would be overpleased at having to travel the roads of Banba during the season of frost and rain. You will have a nice warm stable until the return of spring. You will suffer neither cold nor hunger, however I may fare.

It grieves me to part with that little black ass even for a while. Since the first day I laid eyes on him at the fair of Kinvara, road-weary as I was, I conceived an affection for him. It was not for his colour nor his size nor for his eyes nor his pretty ears nor nice small legs I gave him affection: nor was it for his swiftness of foot, for he never had pace or swiftness – but I think nobody could help being fond of him, because of his 'personality'. He would coax the heart from even a knight of broken pots.

Farewell, my friends, until spring returns, then we shall again hoist our sails and set out through thistle-bearing plains.

I have friends other than those I have enumerated. I have human friends also whom I meet only in seclusion, and alas, I must bid good-bye to some of them also. I had but little opportunity in this booklet to refer to Sean and Peadar and Seamus – three youths whom I used to meet every morning when I was by myself in the wood. They could not afford to delay long with me, because they were compelled to labour to provide for their parents; but while I live I shall remember the feasts we had together in a nook in the wood. Such sport! The stories we used tell each other sitting at the foot of a tree! The voice of the young storyteller, as he told us his story, is ringing in my ears even now –

'At first he was an angel' – I can see his bright eyes sparkling as he said the words – 'an angel who made war on God – but he wasn't cast into hell... he wasn't, because he had done a noble deed long before, and for that he got permission to reside in four places in Ireland.'

And the unbelief evinced by another! How could

such a thing have happened when he had never seen it! I shall nickname that youth Thomas when we meet again.

But farewell, my young friends, until spring comes again.

O knight of the road, is it possible that I shall not see you for the next four months? I am aware that we may, perhaps, meet in the city; but everyone with intelligence knows that the knight of the road one meets occasionally in the city is a different person from the lusty care-free fellow to be seen tramping the wilderness. To know your habits and characteristics, O knight of the road, one must live the wanderer's life with you for a while.

O, noble clans of the roads of Banba, I bid you farewell for a while until the sky clears, until biting winter passes away, until the golden sultry summer comes again – a genial, pleasant Irish summer – farewell.

NEW MERCIER PAPERBACKS

BALLADS FROM THE PUBS OF IRELAND

James N. Healy

The ballads in this well presented book form a cross section of the more widely known songs'which are sung throughout Ireland in the favourite meeting place — the local 'pub'.   *7/6*

ISLANDERS

Peadar O'Donnell

A whole family comes vividly to life in a haunting and quiet drama set on the wild, barren and beautiful islands of the northwest coast of Ireland. The setting seems to be a part at once of the geography of the earth and of the world of imagination.   *5/-*

IRISH SHORT STORIES

Seamus O'Kelly

A selection of short stories by the author of *The Weaver's Grave,* Seamus O'Kelly, whose literary works are now mostly out of print. O'Kelly's books are strongly permeated by his boyhood environment in the west, having a poetic imagery akin to the works of Yeats and Synge.
5/-